Light Up Diwali with Colors

Written By:

Roma Devi Singh

The information and illustrations in this book are intended for educational and artistic purposes only. Readers are encouraged to explore further and consult authoritative sources for religious teachings and interpretations.

Copyright © 2024 LDO Publishing

All rights reserved. No part of this book may be reproduced, distributed, or transmitted in any form or by any means without the prior written permission of the publisher, except for brief quotations used in book reviews.

Om Lakshmi Karo Tu Kalyanam, Arogyam Sukha Sampadam, Mama Shatru Vinashaya, Deep Jyotir Namostute.

We invite you to explore other books in the Divine Colors Series and kindly leave a 5-star review if you enjoyed them!

Oh, radiant Lakshmi Maa, Goddess of wealth, prosperity, and abundance, Shine your divine light upon us, Bless our homes with peace and happiness, Fill our hearts with compassion and wisdom, And may we walk the path of righteousness under your loving grace.

Let's Celebrate

Welcome to an exciting journey into the vibrant world of Diwali! In this book, you'll discover how people celebrate this beautiful festival across the globe, embracing customs and traditions that bring joy and light to every corner of the world. We'll explore the significance of each of the five days of Diwali and learn about the eight forms of Mother Lakshmi, the goddess of wealth and prosperity. Through captivating stories, engaging coloring pages, and fun activities, you'll experience the magic of Diwali and understand why it remains one of the most cherished festivals.
Let's dive in and celebrate together!

The flame of the diya represents the soul or the inner light
that dispels ignorance and darkness

This light signifies hope, spiritual awakening, and the
guiding force of truth

The Eight Forms of Mother Lakshmi

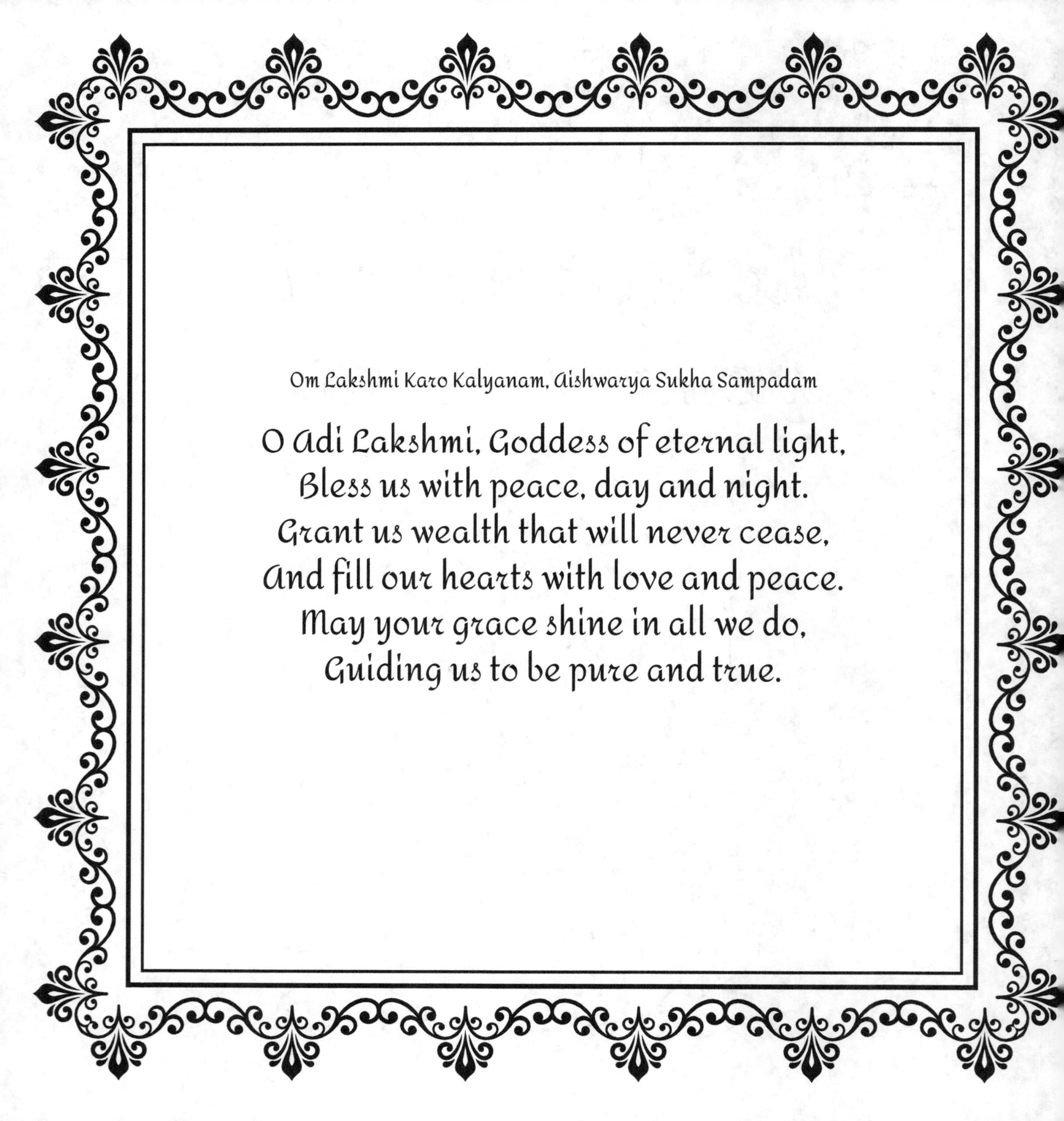
Om Lakshmi Karo Kalyanam, Aishwarya Sukha Sampadam

O Adi Lakshmi, Goddess of eternal light,
Bless us with peace, day and night.
Grant us wealth that will never cease,
And fill our hearts with love and peace.
May your grace shine in all we do,
Guiding us to be pure and true.

Adi Lakshmi

Adi Lakshmi : The Goddess of Eternal Prosperity

Adi Lakshmi is the first form of Goddess Lakshmi, known as the Goddess of Eternal Prosperity. The word "Adi" means "first" or "original", and she represents the beginning of all blessings in the world. Adi Lakshmi is the source of all wealth—physical, emotional, and spiritual—and she helps us live a life full of happiness and fulfillment.

Adi Lakshmi is often shown wearing a bright red dress and sitting on a beautiful lotus flower. The lotus is special because it grows even in muddy water, showing us that beauty and goodness can bloom even in difficult situations. She has four hands, each holding something important: a lotus flower, a flag, a gold pot, and she shows the abhaya mudra—a hand gesture that means "do not be afraid".

Adi Lakshmi is like a loving mother who takes care of everyone. She works with Lord Vishnu, who protects the world, to make sure there is always enough love, happiness, and goodness for everyone. She is the power that helps us feel strong and brave, and she brings balance to everything in the universe.

The blessings of Adi Lakshmi are not just about money and things. She also gives us wisdom and happiness inside our hearts. When we pray to Adi Lakshmi, especially during Diwali, we ask for both the things we need and the courage to be good and kind. She helps us understand that true happiness comes from being thankful, sharing with others, and being the best version of ourselves.

O Dhana Lakshmi, bestower of gold and grace,
Fill our lives with wealth's warm embrace.
Bless our homes with treasures and light,
With abundance pure, steady, and bright.
Teach us to share, and with patience endure,
May your blessings be constant, rich, and sure.

Dhana Lakshmi

Dhana Lakshmi : The Goddess of Wealth

Dhana Lakshmi is the form of Goddess Lakshmi who blesses us with wealth and material prosperity. The word "Dhana" means "wealth", and Dhana Lakshmi provides us with the financial stability and material comforts we need to live a secure life. She represents abundance, and her blessings help us feel comfortable and safe.

Dhana Lakshmi is often depicted wearing golden clothes, adorned with jewelry that symbolizes her association with prosperity and opulence. She holds gold coins that flow from her hands, showing her generosity and her desire to bless her devotees. She also holds a pot full of grains, signifying that her blessings are not limited to money but also include food and resources that sustain life. She stands on a beautiful lotus flower, reminding us that wealth, like the lotus, can grow even in challenging situations.

Dhana Lakshmi teaches us an important lesson—that wealth should be used responsibly. It is not just for our own comfort but also to help others and make the world a better place. During Diwali, people pray to Dhana Lakshmi for prosperity and abundance, decorating their homes with lights and flowers to welcome her blessings. She teaches us that true wealth is not just about accumulating riches but about using them wisely to uplift ourselves and those around us.

Dhana Lakshmi reminds us that material wealth can bring comfort, but it is our actions and generosity that bring true fulfillment. When we share our blessings, we create a world full of love, compassion, and joy, which is the ultimate wealth.

Om Lakshmi Shree Pradayai, Arogya Deep Jyotiye Namostute

O Dhanya Lakshmi, provider of food and grain,
Bless us with nourishment through sun and rain.
Help us to share with those in need,
And guide us to plant compassion's seed.
May your harvest bless us with health each day,
As we give thanks in every way.

Dhanya Lakshmi

Dhanya Lakshmi : The Goddess of Food and Nourishment

Dhanya Lakshmi is the Goddess of Food and Nourishment. The word "Dhanya" means "grains", and Dhanya Lakshmi ensures that everyone has enough food to eat and stay healthy. She provides the grains, fruits, and vegetables that nourish us, giving us the strength and energy we need to live our lives.

Dhanya Lakshmi is depicted wearing green clothes, symbolizing growth, fertility, and the abundance of nature. She holds sheaves of grain in her hands, representing the food and nourishment she provides to sustain life. She stands on a lotus flower, which signifies purity and the nurturing power of nature. Her kind and gentle smile reminds us to always be grateful for the food we have and to respect the resources that sustain us.

During Diwali, people thank Dhanya Lakshmi for her blessings, asking her to continue providing abundance in the form of food and nutrition. She teaches us to never waste food and to share what we have with those who are less fortunate.

Dhanya Lakshmi's presence in our lives reminds us that food is sacred and should be respected. She teaches us that true abundance comes not just from having plenty but from ensuring that no one goes hungry. By being mindful of our resources and sharing with others, we can create a world where everyone is nourished and cared for.

Om Lakshmi Deep Jyotir Devi, Kalyanam Pradayai Namostute

O Gaja Lakshmi, full of strength and grace,
Bless us with courage in life's embrace.
Help us rise with wisdom and might,
And stand tall, guided by your light.
May your power keep us steady and bold,
As we move forward with hearts of gold.

Gaja Lakshmi

Gaja Lakshmi : The Goddess of Power and Strength

Gaja Lakshmi is known as the Goddess of Power and Abundance. The word "Gaja" means "elephant", and Gaja Lakshmi is often depicted with two elephants by her side. These elephants symbolize power, strength, and royal authority. Gaja Lakshmi is the form of Lakshmi who blesses us with courage, success, and the ability to overcome challenges.

Gaja Lakshmi wears red and gold garments, symbolizing power, prosperity, and the regal nature of her blessings. She sits on a lotus flower while the elephants shower her with water, representing the flow of blessings and abundance. The elephants' presence signifies not only material wealth but also the strength and resilience needed to protect and maintain that wealth.

During Diwali, people pray to Gaja Lakshmi for strength, prosperity, and the courage to face life's challenges. Her blessings help us achieve our goals and bring success in our endeavors. Gaja Lakshmi teaches us that true power lies in being kind and using our strength to help others. She reminds us that abundance is not just about material wealth but also about inner strength, generosity, and the ability to uplift those around us.

Gaja Lakshmi's story inspires us to be both strong and compassionate. She teaches us that true abundance comes when we use our power to create positive change, protect those who are vulnerable, and spread blessings to all.

O Santana Lakshmi, protector of family dear,
Bless our children and keep them near.
Grant us joy in every child's smile,
And make our homes loving all the while.
May your grace bless our family tree,
With happiness, love, and harmony.

Santana Lakshmi

Santana Lakshmi : The Goddess of Family and Children

Santana Lakshmi is the Goddess of Family and Children. The word "Santana" means "children", and Santana Lakshmi blesses families with love, joy, and healthy children. She represents the happiness, growth, and unity that family brings into our lives, and she ensures that future generations are blessed and protected.

Santana Lakshmi is depicted holding a baby in her arms, symbolizing the blessings of children and the nurturing aspect of family life. She wears bright yellow garments that symbolize warmth, joy, and the protective love that parents have for their children. Her presence brings a sense of harmony, growth, and togetherness to families.

During Diwali, families pray to Santana Lakshmi for the health, happiness, and well-being of their children. She teaches us that the love within our families is one of the greatest blessings we can receive. Santana Lakshmi encourages us to always take care of one another and to cherish the bonds that keep us united.

Santana Lakshmi's blessings help families grow and thrive, providing them with the strength to face challenges together. She reminds us that the true wealth of a family lies in love, compassion, and the support we give to one another. By nurturing our families and raising our children with love and care, we honor Santana Lakshmi and ensure that her blessings continue for generations to come.

Om Shree Lakshmi Mangalam, Dhanam Pradayai Namostute

O Veera Lakshmi, fearless and true,
Bless us with bravery in all we do.
Help us face challenges with courage and pride,
With you as our guide, always by our side.
May your strength flow in our hearts each day,
Giving us the will to pave our way.

Veera Lakshmi

Veera Lakshmi : The Goddess of Courage and Valor

Veera Lakshmi is the Goddess of Courage. The word "Veera" means "bravery", and Veera Lakshmi gives us the strength to face challenges and overcome our fears. She represents both physical and moral courage, inspiring us to stand up for what is right and protect those who cannot protect themselves.

Veera Lakshmi is depicted wearing red clothing, symbolizing valor, strength, and determination. She holds weapons in her hands to protect her devotees from harm, and she stands on a lotus flower, ready to defend and bring justice. Her powerful stance and confident expression show that she is always prepared to protect those who seek her blessings.

During Diwali, people pray to Veera Lakshmi for courage and strength, asking her to help them stay brave in difficult times. She teaches us that true bravery is not about fighting for power but about standing up for justice, protecting others, and doing what is right, even when it is challenging.

Veera Lakshmi's presence in our lives reminds us that courage comes from within. She inspires us to be fearless in the face of adversity and to use our strength to uplift and protect others. By embodying the qualities of Veera Lakshmi, we can overcome obstacles and create a world that is just, fair, and full of compassion.

Om Lakshmi Shanti Karo, Deep Jyotir Namostute

O Vidya Lakshmi, wise and full of light,
Bless us with knowledge and insight.
Help us learn, with focus and care,
And guide our minds everywhere.
May your wisdom help us grow each day,
Lighting our path in every way.

Vidya Lakshmi

Vidya Lakshmi : The Goddess of Knowledge

Vidya Lakshmi is the Goddess of Knowledge. The word "Vidya" means "knowledge," and Vidya Lakshmi blesses us with wisdom in the arts, sciences, and all forms of learning. She represents intellectual growth, understanding, and the pursuit of truth, encouraging us to seek knowledge to better ourselves and the world around us.

Vidya Lakshmi is depicted wearing a white sari, symbolizing purity, clarity, and peace of mind. She holds a book and a pen, representing education and the pursuit of wisdom. She often stands or sits on a lotus flower, symbolizing knowledge that blossoms within us, helping us rise above ignorance and confusion. Her blessings provide us with the clarity, focus, and insight needed to succeed in both material and spiritual realms.

During Diwali, people pray to Vidya Lakshmi to bless them with wisdom in their studies, careers, and personal development. She teaches us that knowledge is not just about acquiring facts but about understanding the deeper truths of life, cultivating compassion, and applying what we learn for the greater good.

Vidya Lakshmi reminds us that true wisdom comes with humility and an open mind. She encourages lifelong learning, self-improvement, and the sharing of knowledge with others. Her blessings inspire us to explore new ideas, think critically, and always strive to grow intellectually and spiritually.

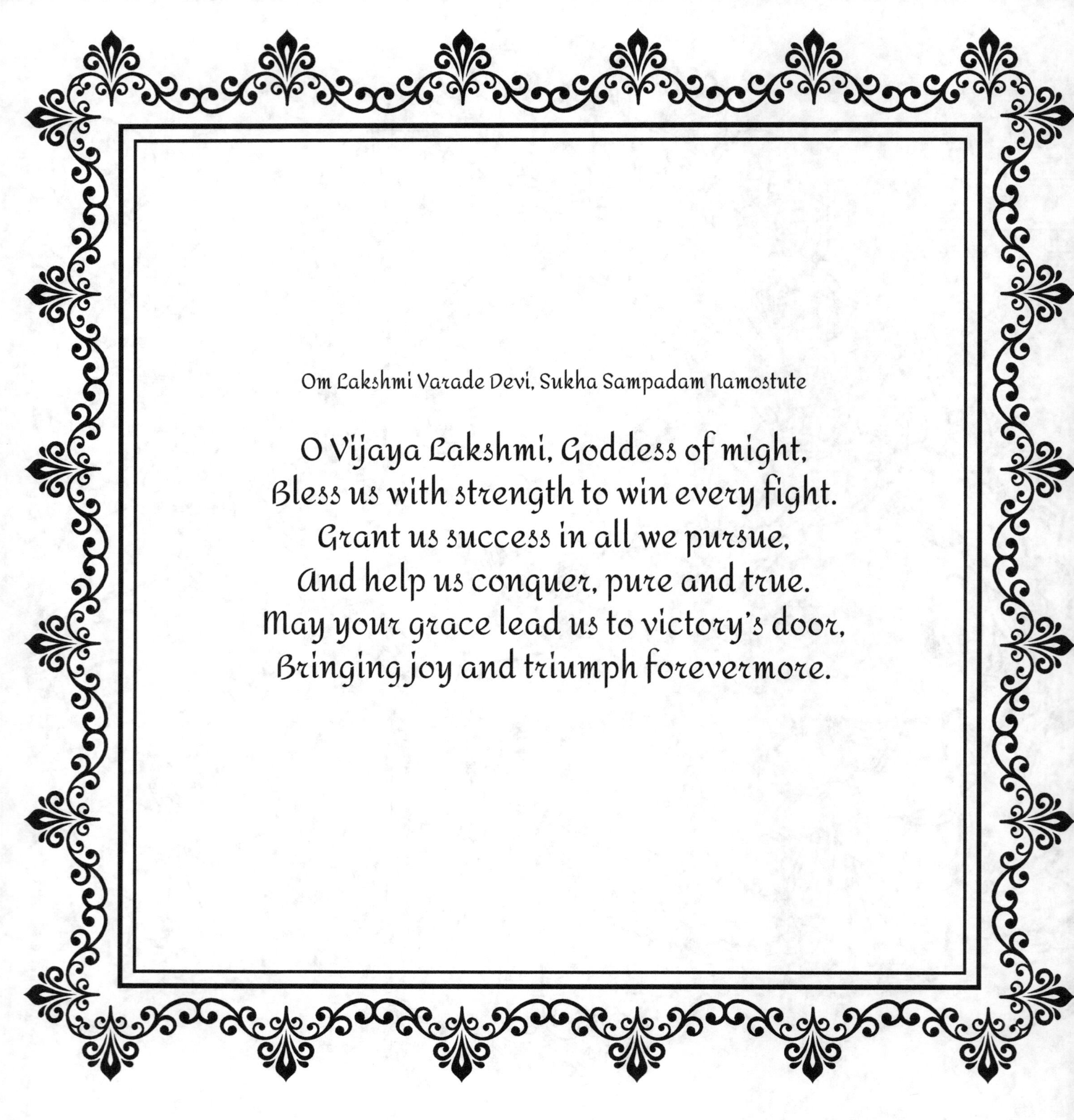

Om Lakshmi Varade Devi, Sukha Sampadam Namostute

O Vijaya Lakshmi, Goddess of might,
Bless us with strength to win every fight.
Grant us success in all we pursue,
And help us conquer, pure and true.
May your grace lead us to victory's door,
Bringing joy and triumph forevermore.

Vijaya Lakshmi

Vijaya Lakshmi : The Goddess of Victory

Vijaya Lakshmi is the Goddess of Victory. The word "Vijaya" means "victory," and Vijaya Lakshmi blesses us with success in all our endeavors. She represents the fulfillment of our goals and dreams, encouraging us to stay determined even when faced with challenges. Vijaya Lakshmi helps us overcome obstacles and reach new heights through hard work and perseverance.

Vijaya Lakshmi is depicted wearing vibrant red garments, symbolizing triumph, energy, and passion. She holds a sword, shield, and lotus flower, representing the tools needed to conquer life's challenges. Seated on a lotus, she embodies the joy of accomplishment and the peace that comes with achieving victory in both material and spiritual pursuits.

During Diwali, people pray to Vijaya Lakshmi for success in their careers, education, and personal goals. She teaches that true victory is not about defeating others but about achieving inner growth and fulfilling our highest potential. Her blessings remind us that with dedication and a positive mindset, we can triumph over adversity and find fulfillment in our journey toward success.

Vijaya Lakshmi inspires resilience, motivating us to celebrate every step forward, no matter how small. With her guidance, we learn that success is not just about the destination but about the lessons learned along the way. Through her blessings, we gain the courage and strength to continue pursuing our dreams and achieving greatness.

The Five Days of Diwali

Day 1 of Diwali : Dhanteras

The first day of Diwali is Dhanteras, a day to celebrate health, wealth, and prosperity. Families buy new things like gold, silver, or kitchen items to welcome good fortune into their homes. It's a time for cleaning and decorating to prepare for the blessings of the festival.

Dhanteras is also considered a lucky day to buy new kitchen utensils

People often buy gold or silver on Dhanteras to bring good fortune

Day 2 of Diwali : Chhoti Diwali

On Chhoti Diwali, or "Little Diwali", people start decorating their homes with bright, glowing diyas (little lamps) and colorful rangolis (patterns made with colored powders or flowers). There's excitement in the air as everyone gets ready for the big day tomorrow!

Lighting diyas during Diwali reminds people of the importance of enlightenment, kindness, and goodness in life

Day 3 of Diwali : Diwali

On this day of Diwali, we celebrate the return of Lord Ram to Ayodhya with his wife Mother Sita and his loyal brother Lakshmana after fourteen years in exile. The people of Ayodhya welcomed them with rows of twinkling lights and oil lamps, symbolizing the victory of light over darkness and good over evil. Today, families continue this tradition by lighting up their homes with sparkling lights and diyas, creating a warm, festive glow. They offer prayers to Goddess Lakshmi, the goddess of wealth, asking for a year filled with happiness, prosperity, and good fortune. Friends and families exchange gifts, share delicious sweets, and enjoy the magic of fireworks lighting up the night sky. It's a day filled with joy, love, and togetherness, reminding us of the warmth and blessings of Diwali.

Day 4 of Diwali : Govardhan Puja

Govardhan Puja is celebrated the day after Diwali. It honors Lord Krishna's protection of Vrindavan. When the rain god, Indra, sent a storm, Krishna lifted Govardhan Hill on his finger, sheltering the people and animals. This puja symbolizes devotion, humility, and respect for nature, reminding us of Krishna's message to value the earth's gifts over pride.

Day 5 of Diwali : Bhai Dooj

Bhai Dooj celebrates the bond between brothers and sisters. According to legend, the god Yamraj blessed his sister Yamuna on this day, promising safety to brothers who receive a tilak from their sisters. Sisters pray for their brothers' well-being, and brothers vow to protect their sisters, symbolizing love and protection.

Around the World

Diwali is celebrated with unique customs in various
countries around the world, each adding its own
cultural twist to the traditional Hindu festival.
Here are some notable customs from different regions

Nepal

In Nepal, Diwali is called Tihar, and it's all about celebrating not just people, but animals too! Every day of Tihar is special because it honors different animals. One day is for crows, one day for dogs, and another day for cows! People decorate these animals with flowers and feed them yummy treats as a way to say thank you for their help in nature. Kids can often join in by making colorful rangoli designs and lighting lamps. It's like a big, happy party for both people and animals!

Singapore

In Singapore, Diwali is super colorful, especially in a place called Little India! This part of the city lights up with sparkling decorations everywhere you look. At night, the streets are glowing with vibrant lights, and you can watch awesome dance performances and try delicious sweets like laddoos and jalebis. Families gather to celebrate together, share sweets, and even visit festive markets. It's a huge celebration that brings everyone together for fun and joy!

Malaysia

In Malaysia, Diwali is known as Deepavali and is a big public holiday. The streets are filled with beautiful decorations, and families create rangolis (colorful designs made from rice or flower petals) at the entrance of their homes. People light oil lamps, bursting firecrackers, and enjoy big feasts with family and friends. In cities like Kuala Lumpur, you can even watch live music and dance shows that bring the whole community together to celebrate!

United States

Diwali has become a huge event in the United States! In big cities like New York, San Francisco, and Houston, people gather to watch Diwali parades, enjoy music and dance performances, and eat lots of yummy foods. In New York's Times Square, they even have a huge celebration with light shows and fireworks. Schools, universities, and even big businesses join in the fun, making it a festival that everyone can enjoy

South Africa

In South Africa, especially in Durban and Johannesburg, Diwali is a time for big gatherings. Families and friends come together for special prayers at temples, followed by cultural performances like traditional dancing and singing. There's lots of delicious food, like curries and sweets, and everyone lights oil lamps (diyas) to bring in the spirit of light and happiness. It's both a religious and social event where everyone enjoys celebrating together

Indonesia

In Indonesia, especially in Bali, Diwali is celebrated by both the Indian community and local Balinese Hindus. Bali is known for its beautiful temples, and during Diwali, these temples are decorated with flowers and lights. People light oil lamps and make offerings to the gods, while kids enjoy fireworks and sweets. The mix of Indian and Balinese traditions makes this celebration extra special and unique

United Kingdom

The city of Leicester in the United Kingdom is famous for its huge Diwali party! They have a Diwali lights switch–on ceremony that turns the streets into a glowing wonderland. There are street parties, fireworks, and even a special Diwali village where you can enjoy music, food, and fun activities. It's one of the biggest Diwali celebrations outside of India, and kids love the exciting firework shows and the chance to explore the festive markets

Diwali Activities

HAPPY DIWALI

Rangoli Design

Color the rangoli accordingly to shape and color

Diwali Gratefulness

Find the Coins

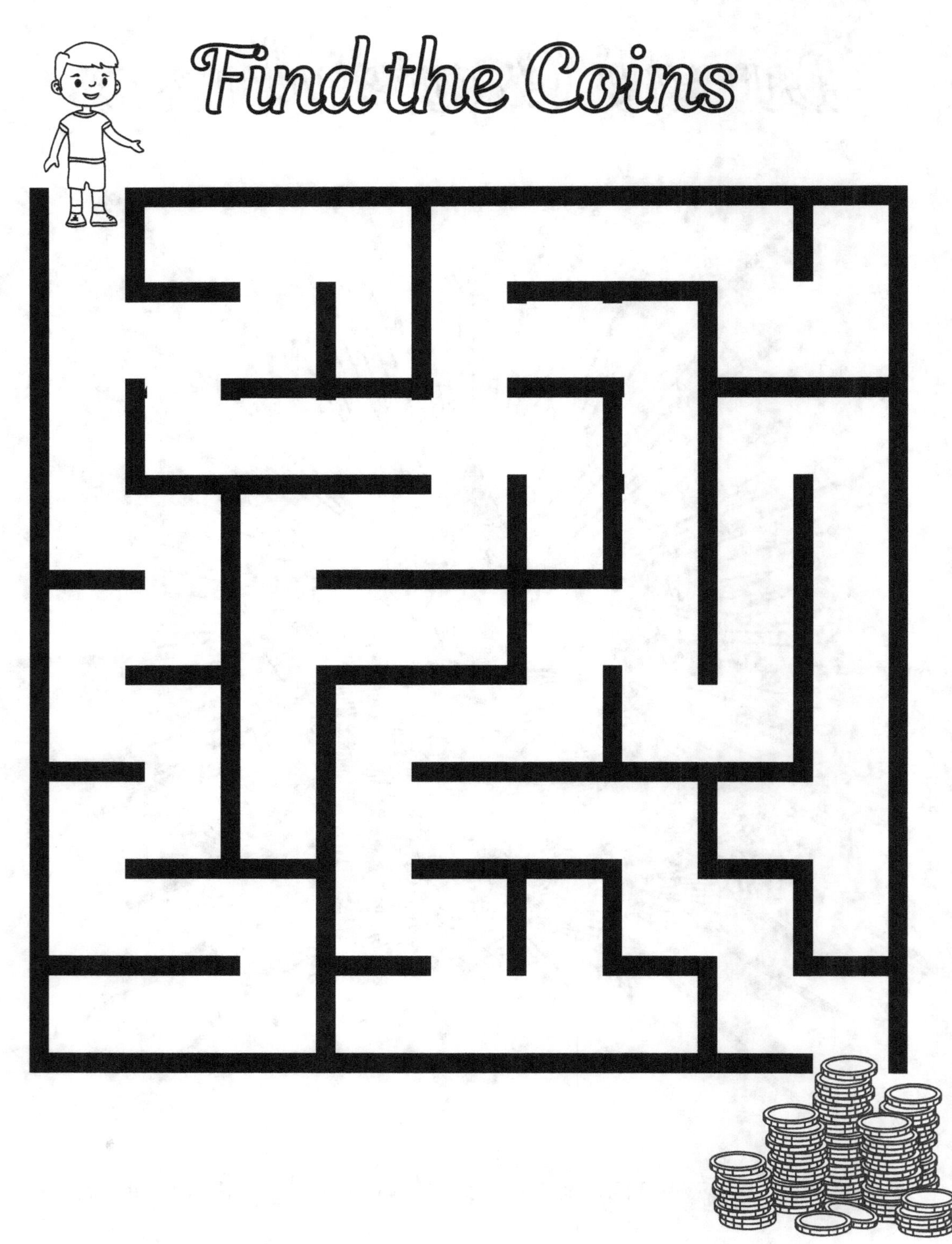

Diya
Connect-the-Dots

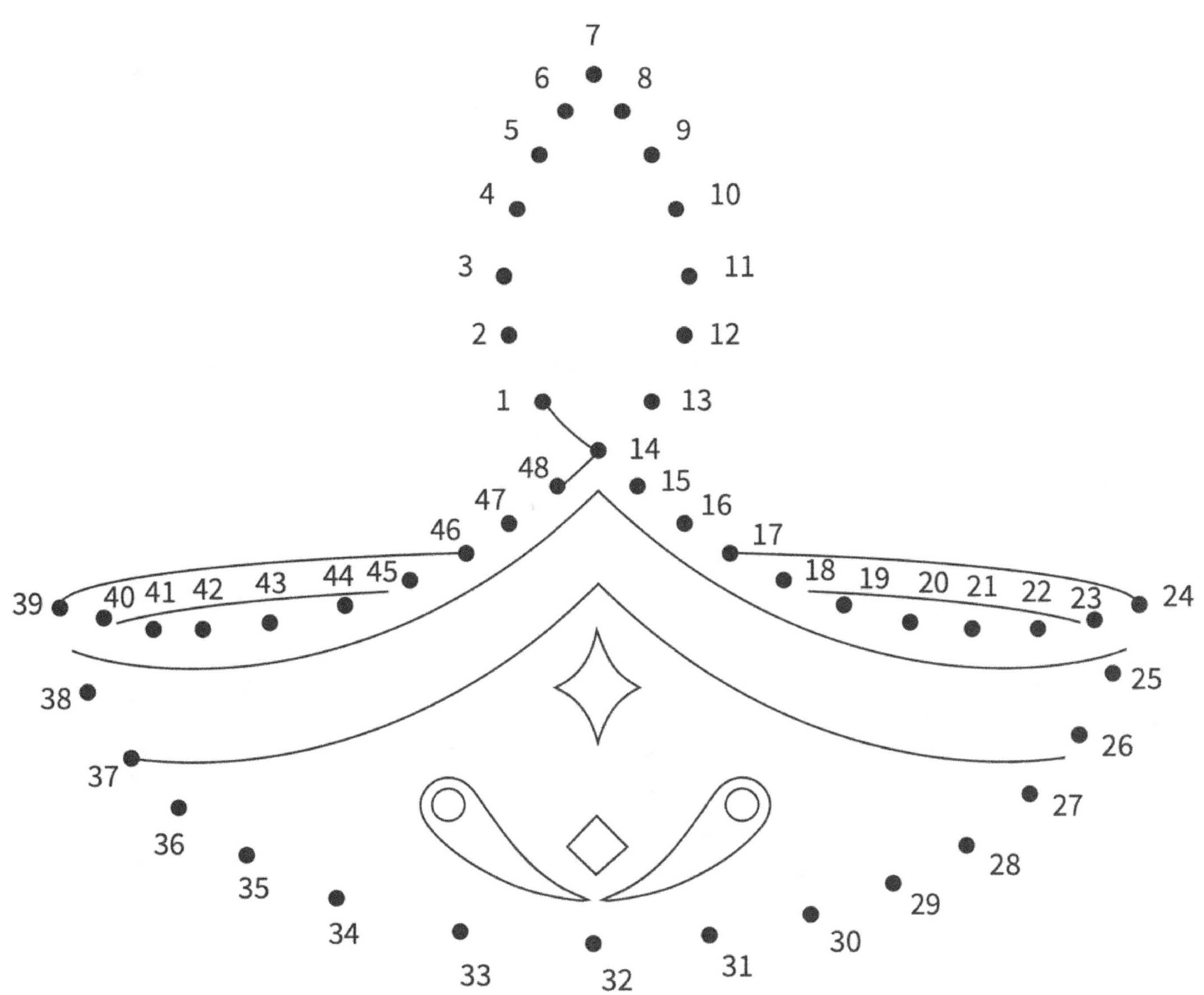

Tik Tac Toe

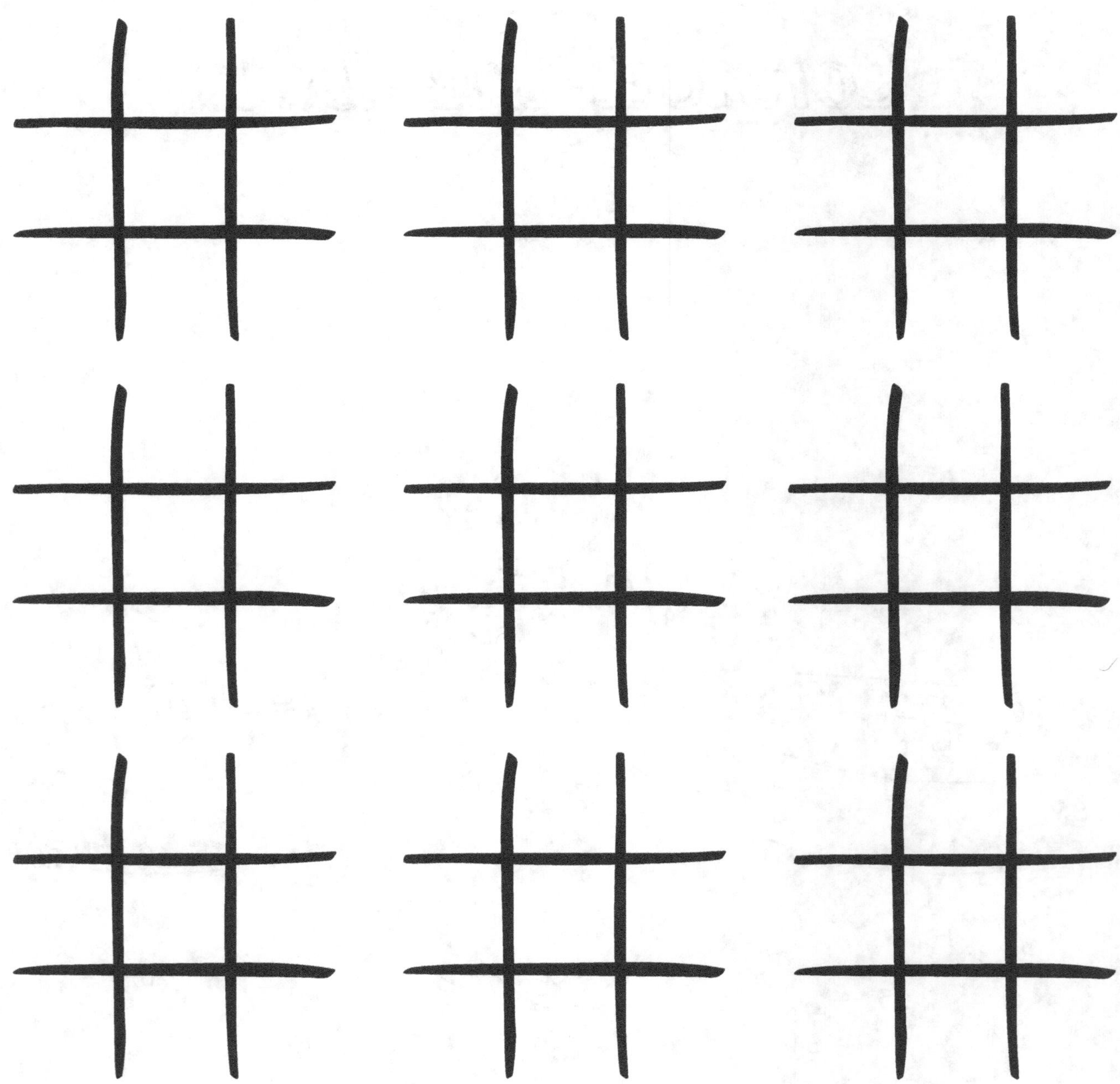

Diwali Word Search

p	o	c	d	k	e	g	h	j	a	y	g	j	d	w
j	u	e	l	e	g	e	i	m	q	c	x	x	i	r
a	s	w	e	e	t	s	n	s	u	a	o	c	y	s
r	m	s	r	a	n	g	d	l	i	r	r	r	a	w
a	g	v	r	k	v	k	u	a	h	v	k	i	n	l
n	l	u	q	f	i	y	r	r	d	x	d	z	f	i
g	s	p	c	m	e	n	a	f	q	d	i	y	a	g
o	p	c	p	l	a	k	s	h	m	i	t	l	d	h
l	r	o	c	a	o	q	s	c	k	w	m	e	v	t
i	y	d	p	p	g	a	q	m	b	a	k	e	p	o
b	k	q	r	e	e	s	o	r	t	l	h	f	j	l
s	u	n	f	l	o	w	e	r	r	i	t	t	m	i
x	s	q	u	i	r	r	e	l	m	f	t	k	o	g
c	e	l	e	b	r	a	t	i	o	n	d	i	w	h
b	j	w	p	r	o	s	p	e	r	i	t	y	l	t

Lakshmi	light	diya
Diwali	prosperity	rangoli
celebration	sweets	Hindu

Color the Firecrackers

www.ingramcontent.com/pod-product-compliance
Lightning Source LLC
Chambersburg PA
CBHW081103300726
48976CB00011B/2714